THE GUN TREE
One Woman's War

THE GUN TREE
One Woman's War

B.K. Zahrah Nasir

OXFORD
UNIVERSITY PRESS

OXFORD
UNIVERSITY PRESS

Great Clarendon Street, Oxford OX2 6DP

Oxford University Press is a department of the University of Oxford.
It furthers the University's objective of excellence in research, scholarship,
and education by publishing worldwide in

Oxford New York

Auckland Cape Town Dar es Salaam Hong Kong Karachi
Kuala Lumpur Madrid Melbourne Mexico City Nairobi
New Delhi Shanghai Taipei Toronto
with offices in
Argentina Austria Brazil Chile Czech Republic France Greece
Guatemala Hungary Italy Japan South Korea Poland Portugal
Singapore Switzerland Thailand Turkey Ukraine Vietnam

ISBN-13: 978-0-19-579504-2
ISBN-10: 0-19-579504-0

Third Impression 2005

Typeset in Hoefler Text
Printed in Pakistan by
Kagzi Printers, Karachi.
Published by
Ameena Saiyid, Oxford University Press
Plot No. 38, Sector 15, Korangi Industrial Area, PO Box 8214
Karachi-74900, Pakistan.

CONTENTS

LIST OF PHOTOGRAPHS

 INTRODUCTION

by

Muneeza Shamsie
Karachi, April 2000

TODAY, Zahrah Nasir is a well-known writer in Pakistan and a contributor to various newspapers, including *Dawn*. She lives with her Pakistani husband in Murree, amid pine-clad mountains and cultivates plants ranging from summer flowers to seasonal vegetables. These tranquil, domestic images belie the remarkable character of the Scotswoman that Afghan Mujahideen named Banafsha-Khomar, who rode with them veiled, and walked across miles of rugged, mine laden terrain with blisters on her feet, while Russian planes zoomed in on the horizon, bringing death and destruction. Her fascinating book, *The Gun Tree*, is an autobiographical account of that journey.

Few women have ever participated in the war alongside the Mujahideen and *The Gun Tree* remains one of the rare eyewitness accounts of that conflict by a woman writer. As such, she lends it a unique perspective and sensibility. More than that, this is also the story of a demoralized divorcee and an erstwhile battered wife on the edge of a breakdown, who found her sense of self-respect and her *being* amid a people of radically different culture and in the heart of a suffering and alien land. The intertwining of this personal journey of self-discovery and her eye witness account of the Mujahideen makes *The Gun Tree* an exceptional book.

Zahrah Nasir, Pam Morris of that time, was twenty-seven when she charged headlong into Afghanistan in 1983. She knew nothing of the country except through travel and adventure books which had captured her imagination, and the press reports of the Russian occupation which had outraged her. She persuaded the Inverness Courier to give her a job, sold her few possessions, and arrived in Peshawar to 'make contact' with the Mujahideen, the Afghan resistance fighters, and go with them to fight the Russians.'

Since then, she had been asked over and over again: *'Why did they agree to take you with them?'*

She had no answer to this, except the immediacy of the words inscribed in her diary. The interpreter had told her repeatedly that the Mujahideen would never take a woman to war with them, journalist or not. But she persisted. The Mujahideen commander received her request with a long silence. She writes:

He didn't move and the silence turned icy.

Then slowly, stretching a leg, obviously immersed in thought, he lifted his head and looked me straight in the eyes.

Arrogance personified, how dare I address him directly?

He stretched his other leg, never faltering in his hypnotic gaze and started to speak in a rolling, sonorous tone.

'Okay,' he nodded, with an almost imperceptible tightening of his lips. 'Okay, pack your bags. We leave in ten minutes.'

I died a thousand deaths in that one second and knew he saw every single one of them flash through my eyes. He shrugged his shoulders and moved to speak again.

I couldn't help it. Something like anger snapped inside my head and the intractable words shot out of my suddenly dry mouth.

'Okay,' I replied. I'll pack my bags. We leave in ten minutes.'

That was the most defining moment in her life.

On the journey across the border, the Mujahideen Commander continued to challenge and test her mettle by offering her the chance to go back to Pakistan, but she refused. Instead, she kept pace with the Mujahideen on foot, at a tremendous pace, half-walking and half-running across the mountains, until the commander rode up to her with the words:

'Yes, you can walk. You have Afghan muscles but you are a woman and here is a horse for you.'

She was evidentially a very good rider too, but nothing had quite prepared her for the terrors before her. Airplanes dived in and dropped bombs, blowing up the mountainsides, setting villages and trees aflame, and leaving behind countless dead amidst screams of the dying and the wounded. In the weeks that followed, Zahrah Nasir learnt that travelling at night was safer and that a beautiful blue sky on a peaceful clear day spelt danger of MiGs and bombs. With the exception of one good meal at the beginning of her journey, she suffered hunger, privation, and dysentery and saw crops and fields burnt by incendiary bombs. The deeper she went into Afghanistan, the more the author saw people with stomachs swollen from starvation and young men with gaping wounds and amputated limbs, or feet blown off by landmines with no medicines to cure them or ease the pain. She was often embarrassed by the faith of people the total strangers—who came up to her and said, 'You will tell the West what is happening here... You can get help for us. You are a journalist...'

Sometimes, she was on the march for twenty-three hours a day. Once, after a particularly long and arduous journey, the Mujahideen camped for the night in a place that was 'straight out of the Wild West'. In her diary she wrote:

> *Taken to a mud and straw shanty, where I slept sandwiched between twelve Mujahideen.*
>
> *Supper was disgusting, a kind of rice stew which even the men couldn't eat.*
>
> *Couldn't get my boots off.*
>
> *Feet too sore and swollen, so I slept with them on.*
>
> *Well... didn't actually sleep.*
>
> *Too hot. Too exhausted, and too scared.*
>
> *It was okay until something slithered into the corner behind me.*
>
> *I didn't know what it was, but fear of the unknown certainly kept me awake.*
>
> *Surviving on nothing but overdrive now.*

I actually found myself walking the proverbial three steps behind the man today, eyes averted, veil firmly in place. Not speaking unless spoken to.

Later, she writes about her journey as one 'into the unmapped, unfathomed realms' of her emotional self and a physical and mental testing ground. She adds:

There was no going back. No turning tail, no seeking solace in self-pity, no question of shedding tears of self-righteous anger.

If I cried now, if I let myself surrender, then that would be it.

I couldn't afford to break...

While the Mujahideen accepted me as a strong woman, one who could walk or ride with them, there would be no problems.

The minute I transformed into a soft, vulnerable female, I was in trouble.

She only met other women a couple of times. Once among a group of nomads who were making their way to safety in Pakistan, and on the other memorable occasion in a small mountain village. There, they crowded around 'Banafsha-Khomar', befriended her, and offered her tea and food, but thought her very curious indeed. Where were her parents, her man, her children?

The extracts from Zahrah Nasir's diary, which are interspersed with her narrative, have an immediacy, a passion, and rawness of language that gives her book its power. Her use of short staccato sentences, often conjure up vivid poetic images, which say much in a few lines:

The half light before dawn.

Steep rolling mountains, green and red.

Vague impressions, misty outlines, each village each hamlet, each single building bombed.

Everywhere, cemeteries.

On the other hand, she captures a very different mood, when she writes in a later extract:

Sentries outlined against the narrow blue ribbon of the sky above, waving down to us, firing shots in the air, true cowboy style.

Ricochet, ricochet, reverberating from cliff to cliff.

Riding up a magical corridor full of butterflies. Blue, red, yellow, orange splashed wings.

The sound of hooves ringing on rock.

In *The Gun Tree*, Zahrah Nasir frequently comments on the fact that she became a complete person, a woman in the real sense, in Afghanistan, because she was accepted for herself, regardless of gender. However, that respect was only extended to her because she earned it, not once, but many times, with her words and her deeds, over and over again. Few would have been offered the privilege to accompany the Mujahideen to their base camp. She was the only woman there. Zahrah Nasir provides a brief but an illuminating insight into that exclusive domain of 1,500 Afghan warriors. She observed them play volley ball or chess, but also learnt how to re-assemble kalashnikovs and fire an anti-aircraft gun. She participated in discussions on war and in the plans for raids and treated ailments and wounds with the few basic medicines she had brought for herself. She also spent much of her time dodging bullets and bombs with considerable bravery.

The title of her book, *The Gun Tree*, is taken from the name she gave the mulberry tree where the Mujahideen would hang their guns and ammunition. She often sat under its shade and it was there that she came to know of an event—the stoning of an alleged spy—which though, was an act of justice to her companions, but was so shocking and totally unacceptable to her that she could not face it. The incident forcibly brought home how vulnerable she was.

She writes:

If I had accepted the reality of the stoning, I would have gone mad.

I know that now, and with this knowledge comes the fact that I was already verging on insanity, when I undertook the journey. I needed to feel this sharp edge, experience shock and fear, in order to shed my manacles and walk free.

The Gun Tree is a story of great, old-fashioned chivalry, of a Mujahideen commander who challenged her, trusted her, became her friend, and ultimately sent her to safety on a day that he knew Armageddon was near. In order to protect them, she neither gives the names of her Afghan friends, nor the areas where they operated, but viewed with hindsight, this gives her narrative a timelessness which takes it beyond the subsequent course of the Afghan conflict, the cynical manipulation of an unhappy country by vested interests and the confusion and terror that beset Afghanistan today. *The Gun Tree* remains a portrayal of the courage and anguish of war, of the moments of great valour and terrible barbarity, which embodies the struggle of so many peoples the world over, winners or losers, throughout the ages.

❧ PREFACE ❧

by

B.K. Zahrah Nasir

GOING to war may be an absolutely ludicrous path to choose as a means of 'escape'. All these years later I can see that but then, it seemed the most logical solution to the situation I found myself in.

A broken marriage, the loss of my two children, a life that was going nowhere except downwards, friends who disappeared into the woodwork and a family who didn't appear to understand the crisis I was in; had all put me on the road to psychiatric care. War came first, psychiatric treatment later!

I'd already had the attention of these 'mind benders' who appeared to want nothing less for me than to conform: To throw away my jeans and T-shirts, start wearing socks with sandals, and dress in nondescript outfits to turn me into one of the faceless masses I have never understood.

A person is a person and I happen to be who I am. Nothing more. Nothing less. Just me.

The psychiatric treatment had been initiated by my first husband, a chauvinist who I was well rid of but, UK law being what it was, having been a patient in a mental hospital I didn't get custody of my children. All sorts of factors drove me to take the decision I did.

The statement sounds rueful but I don't mean it that way at all. Quite to the contrary. Afghanistan. The word still rolls around my mouth like an overlarge marble. The type of amber-eyed glass beauty I prized as a child.

Also, at that time I prized knots.

The complexities of knots are something I learnt at the tender age of ten when, as a member of the Girls' Life Brigade I achieved recognition for my skill. Inordinately proud of my accomplishment, I walked home from class at 8:00 p.m. on a freezing winter night in order to 'flash' the knot badge hastily sewn onto the sleeve of my navy blue tunic. No one saw it. It was too dark and, as a punishment for the dreadful sin of pride, I was further awarded with a thick ear and a cold. However, none of this helped in the slightest when the marital knot came undone! So, back to Afghanistan.

To a country I'd read about, dreamt about, speculated about and sorrowed over since the Russians invaded it with 90,000 troops on 27 December 1979. All too briefly, the western world made a passing reference to the 'unfortunate' invasion of Afghanistan, entering into the spirit of things by a token boycotting of the Moscow Olympic Games in 1980. The mighty American government even went as far as imposing a grain embargo. Halting their supply of wheat to the then Soviet Union as a show of protest which didn't last as it hit their own agricultural pocket far more.

The invasion was also overshadowed, if not overwhelmed, by the 'hostage situation' in Iran which coincided with and overlapped the invasion to such an extent that America failed to note, or to announce, which is probably more correct, exactly what the Russians were up to.

May be the multitudinous American spy satellite network was all wearing blinkers—Afghanistan—who in the West cared anyway?

An early diet of travel and adventure books, (although I still haven't read Kipling), had injected something into my formative being which, instead of remaining 'underground', decided to burst into volcanic activity when I most required a safety valve to blow.

Coincidence? Fate? Whatever one wants to call it. It just happened to come together in 1983 at what was, probably, one of the most difficult periods of my life. I hope I never have to face such a time of sheer desperation again but who knows what would come out of it. Certainly not Afghanistan again. Times have changed. The Afghanistan of my ideals has changed beyond recognition.

It is most unlikely, though not beyond the realms of imagination, that I would choose such a destination now.

How to explain, honestly, what drove me? Actually, I can't. I don't have the right words anymore. I may have had them on the tip of my tongue at the time. I know I justified myself on local radio in the Highland Capital of Inverness. Though I squirm to think of that interview now!

I do know that my family didn't expect to see me alive again. I also know that my time in Afghanistan coincided with the arrest and assassination of two so-called British spies on the Afghan/Pakistan border and that, the day after my return to Scotland, when I went to cover a political conference in Inverness, a fellow journalist almost had a heart attack on seeing me, since presuming me to be one of the alleged spies he'd just filed my obituary! I would love to have seen a copy but never did.

I can say though that two things stick in my mind about preparing for the trip. My preparations took just a few days not weeks. In fact, not two things but three. Firstly, I wasn't quite as far gone as people may imagine as I knew that I would blow every penny in my bank account to get there and, hopefully, back. The capricious life of a freelance journalist meant that, after returning, I would have to wait some time for a pay cheque to come in. With rent to pay, and food a necessity, I had to cover for this.

The Scottish Highlands being a small place, relatively speaking, didn't give me much economic leeway 'but', one of my favourite words it appears and one which readers will learn to live with, yet another coincidence occurred. A sad one for many, an opportunity for me. An extremely rare vacancy, due to the untimely death of a colleague, turned up on a local rag. How dare I belittle it by calling it a 'local rag'?!

The 'Inverness Courier', founded by the Baron family in 1817, was still independently ruled when I knew it but has since been sadly swallowed by a multinational after the demise of my heroine, Miss B. It rarely had more than three reporters, usually two, though, in its heyday it boasted of 'our correspondent' in places such as Khartoum, the Forbidden City and in Kabul. I later read first-hand reports of the two Anglo-Afghan wars. Fascinating stuff! Its claims to fame are many.

Scottish historians and American and Canadian 'root' seekers pore over its precious back copies but the two that stick in my mind are the famous headlines—'Local man lost at sea'—the Titanic had sunk, and if one is to pay attention to the movie 'The Birdman of Alcatraz', then you may notice that a copy of the 'Inverness Courier' lines the bird cage!

Anyway, back to basics. I needed a paying, immediately paying, job to come back to.

The Inverness Courier never in those days, needed to advertise a vacancy. Small though it was, it's reputation was fine and a backlog of applications stretched for miles. It was either exalted or ridiculed, depending on where you stood.

I stood in need of employment, so made a phone call to the then owner/editoress, one Miss Baron O.B.E. a wonderful battle axe few people cared to tangle with.

I knew better than to request a job interview. That would have been fatal.

I would just tell her how much she needed me and what she would miss if she didn't take me on. The height of cheek but worth a shot!

My appointment made, my portfolio under my arm, I drove into Inverness from my Black Isle rented room.

My first port of call though was a travel agent. Just around the corner from the Courier office.

I needed to know the second item on my agenda. The cost of a ticket to Pakistan, in fact, the nearest airport to the Afghan border, plus passport requirements. The travel agent on desk duty couldn't help me.

Package tours fine but...she called the boss.

Carol took me into her personal office to discuss my request.

A long distance Olympic horse-rider herself, she understood the yen for adventure but didn't know where I should fly to.

Eventually, after much poring over of maps and numerous phone calls, Rawalpindi International Airport was decided on with departure in three days time if I got my passport and vaccinations.

She was all set to confirm my seat and even wished she could go with me, particularly if we could throw in a horse-back excursion from Pakistan to Kashgar over the Karakoram Highway but, wait!

I explained that my madcap adventure hung on something else too and that, if successful, I would be back within an hour to confirm my booking.

If I could talk the redoubtable Miss Baron into giving me a job to come back to, then it was a green go. If not, I would have to think again.

Her office, two floors above the old fashioned basement printing press, was straight out of Dickens, herself out of 'St. Trinians' right down to the hockey sticks behind the door.

To cut a long story short, we hit it off and I did such a brilliant sales job that I was employed from the next day!

I explained that I'd booked a holiday first, if she didn't mind. She did, until I was honest enough to tell her where I was going. Her reaction was wonderful.

'Come and meet the other reporters,' she instructed me, darting off down the stairs into the News Room, her sprightly gait belying her age. The two male inhabitants looked askance when she announced I would be joining them, but that first I was going to Afghanistan to fight the Russians and whilst I was there 'Would I get one for her too?'

Miss B was either loved or hated and I could eulogise her, my mentor, forever but this is neither the time nor the place. Suffice it to say that without her, my life today would not be what it is.

Now, I only had to convince my bank manager. What an ogre the word still conjures up but what an angel he was in disguise, though I didn't know it at that time.

Mr Moody. Poor Mr Moody. Long since retired but with my best interests at heart. I had exactly 1,000 pounds in divorce settlement plus a clapped out Volkswagon Beetle. I needed all of it, including the Beetle, to get me to the airport and keep me mobile afterwards.

He councilled against my 'rash decision'. This was a small town where bankers knew everything and he acted in place of my father.

Poor Mr Moody...he didn't stand a chance.

He couldn't prevent me from blowing my money, it was mine after all but he could advise me to invest it. 'The bank will make sure you have a good return but going to war is not the answer'.

'I'd like it half in cash and half in travellers cheques' I told him.

'My dear, you will end up destitute'.

'Mr. Moody, I'll end up being someone you've heard of!'

He surrendered, it was my money after all, though when I had to pay back a future bank loan against a car replacement and didn't have the money, he took it in good stead when I handed him a painting.

'What's this?', he asked.

'One of my paintings' I told him, 'It'll be worth a fortune when I die.' I can't but wonder if he still has it.

So, on a shoe string, or rather sandal strap budget, I was off.

Not bravely, I must admit.

Blindly towards Afghanistan. Towards an incredible experience. A future I couldn't comprehend. A country and a people I couldn't really do anything for except mourn.

I still do.

A country which gave me the guts to face up to myself and grow. Things were never to be the same again and, in the aftermath I discovered that the Highlands of Scotland were no longer home.

I was a refugee.

Two years later—a time of more struggle and hardship—for me, I headed for a job in the Sultanate of Oman for four years during which I met and married the wonderful Pakistani gentleman who is my husband.

This was followed by another, also unsuccessful, try at Highland life before we came to Pakistan, at my instigation. Karachi first, out of necessity, but always with an eye to the mountainous north, where currently we live with our dogs, sheep, orchard and garden with mountains and more mountains wherever we look.

It isn't Afghanistan, though it almost could be.

Someone once said that I'd been born a century or two too late to live the life I wanted. They were wrong.

Someone else, a man in his nineties, once burst into the Courier office a year after I'd been to Afghanistan, and announced that he had travelled over a hundred miles by bus to see me. He was on his way to Iceland for Christmas, spoke to me in Farsi and demanded to know if I was the girl in Michener's *Caravans?* I never knew where he came from or where he went.

Obviously Afghanistan touched him, too.

This majestic country was there for me when I needed it but, if you want to understand, then all I can say is reason, judge, reach your own conclusion, but—never forget—there is always a 'but'.

Zahrah Nasir
Bhurban 2000

THE GUN TREE

We sat in shade,
Shade of a tree,
A mulberry tree
Festooned with guns,
Hung with photographs,
Sad mementoes,
Dead heroes,
The world unsung.

Z. Nasir

I'M not quite sure just when I finally outgrew the painstaking process of sifting sand from the river bed through a borrowed kitchen sieve in search of archaeological treasure which would rival the fabulous tombs of the Pharaohs for a place in the history books.

Neither am I sure when I decided to forgo the questionable pleasures of becoming a nun or Robin Hood, although I have a feeling that the latter died a very sudden death when I twanged my bowstring in the wrong direction and it broke!

There have been so many uncertainties in my life, that to list them is an absolute impossibility, but the one thing that I am sure of is the moment when I finally became a woman.

Was it when I started wearing makeup and bought my first pair of high heels? Was it the first time I made love and enjoyed it? Was it when I gave birth to my first child?

It was none of these things.

I became a woman when I was treated like one and shown respect for simply being who I was. I became a woman the first time I went to war.

I remember the precise moment of my 'becoming'. It was in a decrepit, windowless hotel room in Peshawar, capital of the North West Frontier Province of Pakistan.

The date, and even the time, are ingrained on my memory.

I had just spent three weeks in self-imposed solitude on one of the Summer Isles, off the west coast of Ross-shire. It had been an attempt at pulling myself together after the breakup of a ten-year marriage and the loss of my two young children.

It was a very strange feeling to begin life at the ripe old age of twenty-seven and there was no one to call me 'mummy' anymore. It was wonderful to be free of a perpetual round of broken ribs and fractured skulls but absolute hell to have lost my children.

I had been treated for depression in a mental hospital and thus lost the custody battle.

Fighting off an impending nervous breakdown, I did the only thing I knew how. I ran. Ran to a place where nothing and no one could harm me.

Ran headlong into a situation where I could do nothing but face up to myself.

During those dreadful three weeks I fought things and dreams which don't, and never will exist. I contemplated suicide, and drowned in shades of blacks and blues I had never guessed existed outside the realms of my own imagination.

I started keeping a diary, recording my feelings. It was an attempt at salvation. It is now frightening to read, but one thing that it did for me was to record the most momentous decision I ever made. A decision I don't think could have been reached in a more balanced frame of mind.

The life-changing resolution which emerged from a stormy sea somewhere between the Summer Isles and Achiltibuie, on the last day of July 1983 was that provincial journalism was no longer for me. I would become a war correspondent.

There was nothing left to lose now, except my life, and that had no importance any more.

What followed was an inward and outward journey of terrifying enlightenment which irrevocably altered the core of my being.

A short two weeks later, I flew to Pakistan.

My plan was to travel to Peshawar, make contact with the *Mujahideen*, the Afghan resistance fighters, and go with them to fight the Russians who had invaded Afghanistan on 27 December 1979.

Ostensibly, that was my plan, but in reality I was working blindly. I had no knowledge of where or how to contact the *Mujahideen*, no knowledge of the language, no names, and, frankly, no idea. However, someone 'up there' must have liked me, as contact was quickly made and only a few days after my arrival in Peshawar, I was going to meet 'the man'.

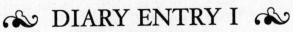 DIARY ENTRY I

Sunday, 21 August 1983
Jans Hotel, Peshawar

THE minute they walked into the hotel I knew that this was it. Something in my guts sank, and I was scared.

Bang on the stroke of 8:00 p.m. Five of them, plus an interpreter. Four with swaggering gait, crossed bandoliers of bullets and kalashnikovs, automatic assault rifles, slung over their shoulders.

Desperate faces, desperate eyes, desperate men.

The fifth one was broken.

Broken and bent with a petrified expression in his glazed, sunken eyes.

I don't know who was more scared, the hotel staff or me. The man with the haunted expression had been captured by the Russians.

They had landed on his farm in helicopters, shot his wife and eight children, then taken him away for interrogation.

He was accused of being a spy for the *Mujahideen*.

They had broken his fingers, his ribs, and torn out his finger nails.

They had left his tongue but he didn't use it.

After weeks of imprisonment, he had escaped and made his way to Pakistan. Now he would go back as a freedom fighter and take his revenge.

The interview couldn't be conducted in the hotel restaurant so, along with two Swedish journalists, we went to an upstairs room.

The four fighters came along. The translator made excuses to the hotel staff before running to join us. The four sat silently in a line along one wall, cross-legged on the floor, while we conducted the interview. I don't know if they understood English or not but they didn't speak, just sat there impassively.

At 9:15 p.m. the interview was over, and after hearing the man's story I certainly didn't want to be a war correspondent anymore.

It had happened to him, it could happen to me.

The interpreter had already told me, over and over again, that there was no way that the *Mujahideen* would take a woman to war with them, even if that woman was a journalist.

For my own peace of mind though I had to ask, there was no danger in this as I'd finally accepted that they wouldn't take me and that was that.

One of them had been paying far more attention to the interview than the others.

A handsome man with a hooked nose, flashing eyes, greying hair, intent manner, and seemingly the right person to answer my pointless question.

'Can we discuss now if you will take me with you into Afghanistan?' I asked him, my heart in my mouth, my soul in my sandals. I had to ask.

Then, at least, I could go home and honestly say they'd refused.

There was fathomless silence.

He didn't move and the silence turned icy.

Then, slowly stretching a leg, obviously immersed in thought, he lifted his head and looked me straight in the eyes.

Arrogance personified, how dare I address him directly.

He stretched his other leg, never faltering in his hypnotic gaze, and started to speak in a rolling, sonorous tone.

I listened to his voice, not his words, after all, he was refusing wasn't he?

No, he wasn't.

'Okay', he nodded, with an almost imperceptible tightening of his lips. 'Okay, pack your bags. We leave in ten minutes.'

I died a thousand, ten thousand deaths in that second and knew he saw every single one of them flash through my eyes.

He shrugged his shoulders and moved to speak again.

I couldn't help it. Something like anger snapped inside my head and the intractable reply shot out of my suddenly dry mouth.

'Okay' I replied. 'I'll pack my bags. We leave in ten minutes.'

He started then, half smiling, sincerely warning me, 'You know that there is a war in Afghanistan. Many people are being killed every day. Women are being killed too. Children are being killed. The Russians come in helicopter gunships, they come in planes and bomb. It's war. You might not come back. You may never see your own country. You may be killed'

He shot his challenge into my head as surely as if it were a bullet from the gun he cradled in his arms and waited.

'I know', was all I could say, though, in retrospect, I didn't know at all. 'I'll pack my bags.'

He looked into my head again, shrugged his shoulders and announced in a tone that brooked no argument, 'You are a woman. You must be sincere.'

I went to pack my bags and in doing so became a woman.

Even now, reading the notes from my diary, I feel resigned to the content of the commander's statement.

All the lectures, the radio programmes, the general discussions which came about after my return to Scotland, all contained the same question, 'Why did they agree to take you with them?'

The commander's words have been repeated so often that in moments of insecurity they come back to me.

I hear them in that particular tone of voice, see them in the resigned shrug of his bullet laden shoulders, and get a certain sense of satisfaction and pride from the words of a stranger through which I 'became'.

⮌ DIARY ENTRY II ⮌

Tuesday, 23 August 1983
Peshawar – Parachinar

TRAVELLING to war on the front seat of a hired coach, which trailed tinsel ribbons, and bells from fenders and roofrack, with the added unreality of paintings and fancy metal work on every square inch of bodywork, I contemplated the boxes of mines pushed under my seat, the hand grenades in the luggage rack, the guns and the twenty-four desperadoes sitting behind me, and told myself, 'It'll be okay, you're a woman now with four bodyguards to boot!

A man wouldn't get four bodyguards, would he? A sexist attitude but nevertheless a fact which certainly made me feel more secure.

'You die before she dies', they were told, although that made me feel uncomfortable.

Who was I anyway?

DIARY ENTRY III

Wednesday, 24 August 1983
Terra Mangal

WE rode the bus to the border, got our caravan together, and headed through a 16,000 foot high mountain pass. The road went straight up and I wondered how I was ever going to make it. This was only the beginning.

❧

Disguised as an Afghan in *shalwar* (baggy trousers) and *kameez* (longshirt) with my black veil blowing in the wind, I perched on top of a pile of anti tank missiles, which were, in turn, strapped to the back of a protesting horse. I tried to wedge myself securely in place, between sacks of hand grenades and other weaponry. At first, I thought I would have to walk like everyone else, and set off up the mountain, carrying my small back pack of sleeping bag, camera, notebooks, a few clothes, and toiletries.

The commander galloped up behind me, leapt off his mount and said, 'You can walk'. A statement not a question. 'It is a long walk.'

'I can walk,' I told him, remembering a hundred Scottish moors and mountains, in snow, wind and rain.

'It is not too late, you can go back to Peshawar,' he grinned, offering me a way out.

'I can walk,' I repeated through gritted teeth, and continued marching up the track, dodging descending camels, a never ending procession of refugees, and wondering just how far we were actually going.

I had thought that I was going to be smuggled into Afghanistan through a quiet mountain pass, but this particular pass resembled Piccadilly Circus at rush hour. Even now, I find it hard to comprehend just how many hundreds and thousands of people are still pouring over that mountain, in a surging tide of agony and despair.

Going down, injured, legless, armless, men, women and children wearing their grief and desolation for all the world to see, if it dared to look, or, if it cared to see.

Going up, the resistance fighters, the *Mujahideen*, facing death with smiles of pride carrying, along with their guns and ammunition, a raging fire of burning anger.

I struggled up the mountain side, determination in every aching muscle. I would make it. I could walk. I would not fall behind.

The *Mujahideen* were used to traversing this terrain, it was their country, and they were fit. They set a gruelling pace, half run, half walk, half sure that this woman would hold them back.

It was so hot. I felt like an Eskimo who had been stuffed into a microwave and was too relieved to argue when the commander galloped up behind me dragging a baggage horse.

'Yes, you can walk,' he laughed. 'You have Afghan muscles but you are a woman and here is a horse for you.'

Three things happened as we crossed the border. First, I was spotted by the border police and the *Mujahideen* had to bribe them to let me continue. It was either that or me getting hauled off to jail and waiting for the British Embassy to come and bail me out. If that had happened, it would have given me the perfect escape route, but it didn't.

The bribe paid, we galloped across the border like the 'Hole in the Wall' gang of western fame, rifles firing in the air, much whooping and cheering, smiles, and singing.

I didn't realize at that time that they were singing religious songs or I might have been a little more apprehensive.

While all this was going on, the erstwhile commander galloped alongside me and happily yelled, 'Welcome to Afghanistan. Welcome to our country. Now you are an Afghan woman, Pam. Now you are a true Afghan, and your name is Banafsha-Khomar.'

He galloped in front yelling to everyone 'Banafsha-Khomar. Banafsha-Khomar.' They laughed too, and fired another volley of shots into the air.

They whooped and yippee-ed some more, galloping back one at a time to say, 'Welcome to Afghanistan Banafsha-Khomar. Welcome home.'

Hilarity turned to caution.

Within seconds, their eyes scanned the sky.

Horses whinnied and laid back their ears.

The stream of refugees heading for the border paused momentarily, then trekked on.

Then I heard it too.

Planes.

MiGs to be precise.

It was a bombing run. The whole mountainside exploded around us.

Giant cedar trees disintegrated into matchwood.

The horses galloped onwards.

The refugees walked towards safety.

The border was an endless mile away.

There was nowhere to run, nowhere to hide.

Everyone continued towards their destinations.

Some to Pakistan, some into Afghanistan and some, I saw, to their eternal abode.

It was over as fast as it had begun.

The acrid smell of explosions, the flames of burning trees, the crying of terrified children, the wailing of new widows, the sobbing of bereaved men... But no one stopped, everyone kept moving.

I was in shock.

I kept moving too.

❧ DIARY ENTRY IV ❧

Wednesday, 24 August 1983
Afghanistan

D OWN the mountain, through farmland, corn, and potatoes. Getting a sore bum from jolting on the horse.

7.00 p.m.

Halted for the night.

The village is still burning from a bombing raid.

Were those the same planes that bombed us?

Was I a doctor? The people wanted to know.

Did I have any medicine?

I was ashamed that I was only a journalist, but they still seemed pleased.

'You will tell the West what is happening here', they said. 'You will tell them the truth. Tell them we need doctors and medicine. Tell them we need help. Tell them we are their brothers and we will help them if they need it. You can get help for us. You are a journalist.'

I was embarrassed by their faith in me, and even more embarrassed when they insisted I sleep in a good house, with a good roof, one that hadn't yet been damaged. I was embarrassed when they brought food for me to eat. It was the best of what little they had. I was embarrassed when one man brought a bowl of warm, fresh milk from his own cow, then immediately rushed off for another bowl saying, 'This is from the neighbour's cow. See if it is as good as ours.' Pride. Yes. They have pride.

That night I feasted on a small portion of meat stew, *nan* (flat, round, baked bread), honey, and milk.

I never had the luxury of a full meal again during my journey.

We survived on tea, *nan* bread and more tea, and more *nan*. Sometimes, there was no flour for the *nan*.

The further I travelled, the more swollen the people's stomachs were, swollen from hunger, not gluttony.

12 February 1989
Kilcoy, Scotland

It is only now, almost six years after this particular journey, the world is beginning to acknowledge the shortage of food in Afghanistan, and as I write this, 12 February 1989, emergency airlifts of food are finally in the offing.

I can't help but wonder how many more would have survived if help had arrived sooner.

❧ DIARY ENTRY V ❧

Thursday, 25 August 1983
Afghanistan

1 :oo a.m. Awakened by a thunderous hammering on the door. I thought the Russians had come again and was too scared to move.

Bodyguards reassured me that it was okay. It was time to get moving again as we had to cross a vast open plain before daybreak.

Back on the horse, full moon, mountains in the distance, their towering peaks seemingly holding us safe.

On the outskirts of the village women were working in the fields.

It was safer than during the day.

The helicopters didn't fly in the dark.

It all seemed pointless anyway, as once the crops began to ripen, and stomachs gurgle in anticipation of fresh food, the Russians would come, drop incendiary bombs, and leave burning fields behind them.

The women would watch, calculating: how long to re-plant, how long to re-grow, and how long until the helicoptors returned.
A vicious circle.

Eerie travelling this way, picking our way through river valleys, steep, dark passes with tumbled boulders, here and there the ghostly outline of a purple silver thistle...like home.

Sometimes, we walked, as it was too steep, with too much sliding scree to stay on horseback.

Discovered that part of the plain we had crossed had been a minefield! There was a new stretch of mines up ahead.

The horse in front of me stepped on one.

Its rider was blown into pieces.

An arm flashed in front of my face, the full moon illuminating the atrocity.

I must be having a nightmare.

This can't be happening.
This can't be real.

6:00 a.m. We stopped at a remote tea house, a humble *chaikhana* of adobe and cedar wood.

I drank green tea, then fell asleep on the dirt floor.

An hour later, we set off again.

The half-light before dawn.

Steep rolling mountains, green and red.

Vague impressions, misty outlines, each village, each hamlet, each single building bombed.

1. A remote *chaikhana* .

Everywhere, cemeteries.

Long poles of wood stuck in the ground, topped with waving strands, and streamers of new brightly coloured cloth, or old faded tattered remains of fluttering banners.

More refugees. 'Thank you for coming to our country. Thank you for your help.

Help? What help? I was hanging on to my horse and dreaming a living nightmare. What help was that?

We travelled until 7:00 p.m.

At one point, my mount's load slipped sideways, and I with it. A bodyguard jumped to catch me, to break my fall, as he did so, the butt of his rifle swung underneath his arm and hit me hard on the side of my head.

I saw stars.

I've no idea how far we've walked or ridden today.

Blisters on blisters, aches on aches, and an exceedingly numb bottom.

An effort to remain conscious.

Thoughts and half-thoughts which have no place here keep flitting through my brain.

Matthew. Jennifer. My children. Will I ever see them again?

Have they been taught to hate me yet?

Three weeks ago I was in Scotland.

Three weeks ago I had been trying to find some form of sanity in the Summer Isles.

Three weeks ago I had decided to do something with my life.

Three weeks ago I had decided to be a war correspondent.

Three months ago I had been a battered wife.

Three hours from now I'll be asleep.

Three hundred miles from here I'll be safe.

Three seconds from now I might be dead.

I was under the impression that tonight was going to be spent in another village and I made up my mind to ask for water to wash but no question of that here.

The camp for this night is right out of the Wild West.

There seem to be lots of men here, no women except me, but I'm safe.

Taken to a mud and straw shanty, where I slept sandwiched between about twelve *Mujahideen*.

Supper was disgusting, a kind of rice stew which even the men couldn't eat.

Couldn't get my boots off.

Feet too sore and swollen, so I slept with them on.

Well, didn't really sleep.

Too hot. Too exhausted, and too scared.

It was okay until something slithered into the corner behind me.

I didn't know what it was, but fear of the unknown certainly kept me awake.

Surviving on nothing but overdrive now.

I actually found myself walking the proverbial three steps behind the men today, eyes averted, veil firmly in place, not speaking unless spoken to.
And so the journey continued.

Always one more mountain to cross, until the day when there were three more mountains to cross, and I knew we were finally getting somewhere.

Although by that stage, I was hardly conscious enough to care.

Hanging grimly on to my horse and its cargo of death, I slipped into a film script, disassociating myself from the entire situation.

There was a woman on a horse who vaguely resembled me but I wasn't there. I was watching the film rolling on and on from somewhere else altogether.

The wheezing sigh of overhead MiGs, the chop, chop, chop of approaching helicopter gunships, the echo of close and distant bombing, occasional bursts of gunfire, voices calling out in a strange language, the thud of hooves; all were a dull backdrop to something I had no option but to hang on to and endure.

It was this test of endurance which made me realize the seriousness of the situation.

I was on a journey, one of those adventures I'd read about so avidly as a child.

But this expedition was far more than a journey across a foreign country, far more than traipsing off to war with a group of heavily armed resistance fighters.
Above all else, this was the journey of a lifetime.

A journey into the unmapped, unfathomed realms of my emotional self.

It was both a physical and a mental testing ground.

A real testing ground rather than the 'familiar' solitude of the Summer Isles.

Here I wasn't on a self-chosen battlefield where all I had to do, if it got too much, was turn tail and run.

This battlefield was quite a different matter.

There was no going back, no turning tail, no seeking solace in self-pity, no question of shedding tears of self-righteous anger.

If I cried now, if I let myself surrender, then that would be it.

I couldn't afford to break.

I couldn't afford to let anyone here see my weakness.

This wasn't pride, it was self-preservation.

As long as the *Mujahideen* accepted me as a strong woman, one who could walk or ride with them, there would be no problems.

The minute I transformed into a soft, vulnerable female, I was in trouble.

I needed them and they would only respect a strong person not a weakling who would get in their way.

This journey into myself was an endurance test beyond all my known limits.

❧

Long winding corridors lined with the faces of my past, and present, faces I could only surmise belonged to my future, if I had one.

This really was the survival of the fittest on so many planes at once, each plane being further confused by a myriad angles.

The gruelling pace at which we travelled, often for as much as twenty-three hours a day, interspersed by fifteen-minute breaks for tea and *nan*, or just tea, freed the mind from its body shell and spun it far out into space.

The endless scrambling up and down sheer mountain sides, crawling along goat tracks, precariously drawn around the sides of steep cliffs, where heavily laden donkeys over-balanced and fell with bloody, crashing thumps to boulder-strewn earth 500 feet below, all served to wrack the body with the searing birth pangs of the real self, the previously unknown self, which was fighting to be born.

The donkeys screamed as they fell. A high-pitched wailing scream which shattered the nerves and pierced the eardrums. A final bloody thud and, if possible, a short, sharp shot, then silence. It would have been the same for any of us, and all of us, without exception, accepted this. There was nothing else we could do.

The morning of our last day on the trail began as usual at 1:00 a.m.

We had had only one hour's rest.

DIARY ENTRY VI

Friday, 26 August 1983
Afghanistan

I N the light of the moon, saddle sore and weary, I waited for the convoy to get underway.

The commander said that there were three more mountains to cross and that one of these was very high and difficult.

I nodded my head.

I was way past smiling, and I was feeling ill.

Breaking out into a cold sweat despite the scorching heat, I am trying hard to ignore the painful stomach cramps which have been threatening to blank me out since the previous day.

We reached the first mountain in the misty light of a pearly dawn.

Our convoy had broken up into small groups of six for safety.

Countryside more and more arid. Riverbeds dry and rough, no more fertile valleys around.

I climbed the steep mountainside on foot, dragging my horse behind me.

I was in danger of falling asleep, only the need to stay alive kept me moving.

2. Part of the *powindah's* flocks.

In ethereal swirling mist on the mountain summit we met a large caravan of nomads, *powindahs*.

They were heading back the way we had come.

Unveiled women, high cheek bones, colourful clothes and jewellery, hair in dozens of small plaits, bursting with pride in each effortless step that they took.

A group of ten women stopped mid-stride when they saw the filthy, exhausted apparition that was me.

They stared in silence for a few moments, looking me up and down, inside and out.

&

Then they spoke in softly lilting voices, sounding Gaelic, gestured towards their camels, then pointed towards the distant mountains in the general direction of Pakistan.

I think they may have been asking if I wanted to go with them.

Go with them to safety.

It was tempting, but I shook my head, smiled as best I could, gritted my teeth, and marched on, still dragging my horse.

Tiny *powindah* children bounced from rock to rock, in imitation of the goats they were herding, and tall, princely men sang as they floated along through the mist.

They were a beautiful people.

We began to make the treacherous, stumbling descent, and the majestic people, with their bleating goats, and supercilious beasts of burden, sailed quickly away into the wreaths and spirals of rose tinted mist.

Within minutes, all that was left of this fleeting encounter were the dulcet tones of a spiritually hypnotic song, drifting along the vaporous tide.

Slowly, even this turned to silence.

A book I read about customs in Afghanistan before I came here said that to pass wind was a dire insult. Someone forgot to tell the horses that as the strenuous uphill climb and the straining muscles involved had them passing wind at every step!

I was fast reaching the end of my tether. Could I push myself a little bit further?

The inward-outward journey was becoming too much to take.

The diversity of emotions, of up and down mountains, of smiling, tranquil people, the desolation of the homeless, the suffering, the pounding of bombs, the chop, chop, chop of approaching helicopter gunships, bright laughter carried on waves of lavender scented air.

Contradictions.

Peace and war.

War and peace.

Each separate, singular emotion encapsuled within the same fragmentary blink of the same fragmentary moment.

❧

Now we travelled along a thin ribbon of valley, grey with dust and boulders, brightened by a vast ocean of fragrant lavender.

The sky was blue, cloudless, and perfect, the blue of cornflowers and morning glory.

The blue of my clothes, shalwar and kameez, the startling blue of my inner emotions.

Someone once told me that blue is the colour of the higher realms of spirituality.

Here, at this precise moment, a particle frozen in time, everyone's aura was blue.

Even the bombed homes and farmsteads appeared to be painted static shades of blue.

Suddenly, out of nowhere, a spring welled up inside me.

Everything was so blue and newborn that I wanted to cry.

The commander galloped up on his blue white horse, flashed blue white teeth from a navy blue growth of unshaved beard, and said, 'Afghanistan is very beautiful,' I agreed. 'This is a beautiful day. No clouds, only sun, the sky is so blue and clear'.

He gestured with open arms, flung them wide, encircling all horizons.

'Blue' he said. 'Clear' he said. Then in a sombre tone, 'Blue weather. Perfect weather for helicopter gunships. They will come. They will see us and then they will bomb-bomb.'

He galloped away and the blue changed colour.

I stopped admiring the scenery and began instead to plot my course of action when the helicopters came.

Should I gallop for the trees, if there were any?

Should I jump off my horse and make for the boulders in the riverbed?

Or, if caught in the open, should I dive for cover in the rolling purple-blue lavender bushes?

I was dressed in blue.

It would be camouflage and, if I died, then at least my last memory would be of fragrance, not fear.

I decided on the latter, even if it did mean abandoning my horse, which would undoubtedly flee, leaving me to walk or crawl to my final destination.

I galloped after the commander and asked him what would happen if the Russians caught us in the open.

'We are strong. We have many weapons. We will fight,' he said.

That wasn't what I meant, but I had long since learnt that a direct question, rarely, if ever, resulted in a direct answer. Sometimes, I think, because no one would have liked the answer.

I wasn't the only one needing to prove my strength in order to survive.

Two mountains later, we came to a remote hamlet, or rather, what was left of it.

I dismounted stiffly and thankfully from my shattered mount, and hobbled up boulder strewn steps to a courtyard shaded at one end by a piece of rattan supported by stout sticks.

The crowd of roughly thirty men parted in front of me like the waves parting before Moses, and I was far too exhausted to notice the reason why?

'Hey. How're you?' drawled a deep American voice.

Surprised, to say the least, I studied sunglasses, a bearded, hatted American face, a camera hung neck, notebook, who was sitting by the extremely amused commander.

Joke over, I was led away by the village headman while the bona fide Reader's Digest war correspondent stayed where he was.

I followed the thin, wrinkled, smiling headman up a steep hillside to a cluster of mud hovels.

A shock of grey hair bounded happily in front of me and every few steps he turned, twinkling grey eyes set in a pock marked face, to see if I was still there.

After seating me on the remains of a mattress in a shaded corner, he promptly disappeared, a small figure in green shalwar kameez and striped waistcoat, hurrying back to the courtyard of men. Angry at being secluded from the men but too tired to do anything about it, I promptly fell asleep. I don't think I slept very long, my stomach wouldn't let me, but when I finally opened my eyes it was with the utmost amazement. While I had slept, nineteen women and as many children sat around

3. In the village of women and children.

me in a half circle and yet more peeped, giggling, from corners.

The look of surprise registering on my face when I saw them provoked absolute hysterics.

Some of the women hid behind their veils, but when I pulled my own veil away to grin at them, then quickly pulled it back into place, they forgot their shyness and laughed uproariously.

I was dumbstruck by the classic beauty of their finely chiselled features. Brown, grey, and hazel eyes, inquisitive, friendly, carried a wish that we communicate in one way or another.

A mixture of sign language, English, which they didn't understand, the few words of Persian that I had learnt, plus drawings in the sand, resulted in a meal I didn't want but which would have been impolite to refuse.

They insisted I eat, while they ate nothing.

Afterwards, it was time for tea.

Would I have *tor chai* or *sabz chai*, black tea or green? Tea leaves were produced to explain the difference. How could I drink tea without sugar?

I tried to tell them that I didn't want food as my stomach was sore, the nearest I got to was rubbing my stomach, and then my forehead, and saying sick.

Eventually, realisation dawned upon them, as one of the headman's two wives rubbed her own stomach whilst calling for her previously banished children.

Obviously, I must be in the same state as she, pregnant, therefore, no matter how sick I felt, food was the answer.

They wanted to know my name, the country I came from, the name of my village, where my parents were? Where was I going? and why?

The one word of reply that they understood was journalist.

Aah. But was I married, where was my man, my children?

How could I tell them? How could they possibly understand?

One of the little girls picked up my camera and her mother handed it back, gesturing to ask what it was. I pointed to it and pretended to click.

The headman re-appeared like the genie in the lamp, turban askew and teeth flashing.

He knew what a camera was.

He had seen one in Pakistan.

His women and the other women here had never left Afghanistan, never left their village, never seen a white woman before, let alone a camera.

What he told them, I can only guess, but they all lined up to have their photographs taken.

These photographs (I have only four of them) are the most precious of my career.

As I clicked the shutter I felt it.

I said goodbye to the women, wishing I could stay with them forever.

They are my sisters.

The headman walked with me to the top of the hill where the Mujahideen had re-assembled.

I walked towards them with tears in my eyes for things that could have been but would never be.

A voice called after me.

A young girl, purple veil fluttering in the breeze.

'Banafsha-Khomar.' she called.

'Mujahid', then she ran away giggling.

The final mountain loomed into sight. It went on and on, upwards, forever.

It was a desert mountain, a mountain of sand, dust, rock, stones, dry gullies, scree slopes, hot sun, and lavender.

The next few hours were nothing short of torture.

I either hung on to my horse or hauled it behind me and felt more sick.

I needed water.

I needed medicine.

I had neither.

After the up, came the down, and that was ten times worse.

Then, out of nowhere, riders appeared from the depths of a cloud of choking dust which rolled towards us.

Hugs, handshakes, and cheers all round.

I gathered that they had ridden out from the base camp to meet us.

☙

We were almost a week overdue, and they had been on the verge of giving us up for dead.

The commander was handed a chestnut stallion which glittered and gleamed in the sun, strong muscles rippling under the sheen of its coat.

He galloped around the convoy waving his kalashnikov in the air, the stallion prancing in high spirits.

The pair paused on top of a rugged outcrop of sand and coarse grass, the stallion reared, and the commander shouted something over his shoulder.

I didn't hear what he said as my knackered old horse suddenly exploded in a frenzied burst of energy and took off after him.

I clung on, bodyguards in mad pursuit and, as the baggage began its inevitable sideways roll, I leapt off trying a professional roll to safety.

That's what they do in the movies!

I hit the mountainside in a breathless bundle and the day turned blue again, this time with stars.

When I came to a split second later, it was to see my horse galloping in mad circles, head down, hind legs up and baggage underneath its belly. A rocking horse gone nuts.

I had visions of anti-tank missiles exploding and hand grenades going off in unison.

The commander came charging back, berating the bodyguards for allowing this to happen, and asking if I was okay.

I was.

Even if my back was broken I had to be okay.

It was many hours before we reached the camp.

The last part of the journey passed in heat filled oblivion.

My bodyguards had finally seen through my Oscar deserving act and knew how ill and exhausted I was.

'Just round the corner, just round the corner', they kept repeating. The corner went on forever.

Along a dry riverbed, through trees, lying delirious over the horse's neck.

Mosquitoes, empty bomb cases, shrapnel protruding from trees and house walls, feeling worse, if that was possible, when I heard voices talking about 'bomb-bombs' and yet more 'bomb-bombs'.

It was late afternoon turning into evening when we followed the glow of a small camp fire into a courtyard, full to capacity with men.

Some I knew, some I didn't, but I didn't care even if it was full of the Russians.

All I wanted to do was sleep.

4. Burnt alive.

I was too ill to drink tea by this time, and crawled after a lantern swinging man, into the depths of a flea-ridden mattress, balanced precariously on the rotting strands of a rope bed.

&

I think I passed out.

I awoke with a jump.

How long had it been? Minutes? Days? All I knew was that the sound of anti-aircraft fire was ripping the half light to shreds.

It couldn't have been long or it would have been dark.

My bed was on a rooftop and, as I opened my eyes, I saw a plane high in the sky, directly above me.

If it dropped a bomb now it would land right on top of me.

Boom.

Finito.

&

Where I got the energy from, God alone knows, but within a split second I was out of bed and running, heart pounding, blood beating a tattoo in my temples, I crouched in the lee of a wall, trying to catch my breath.

The burning fluid soaking my trousers had nothing to do with me.

The plane was still there.

The men were still talking and laughing down below in the courtyard.

I had dysentery.

I crawled back to bed sucking a mouthful of stomach tablets, praying that I wouldn't cough as I didn't have any more clean trousers.

ھ

March 1989. Kilcoy, Scotland

There were approximately 1,500 men in the valley and me. I have chosen not to name it, the commander, or any of the other *Mujahideen*, as the war continues and names can mean death. I don't want to betray the men who were my protectors and brothers.

The women in the remote mountain village and their children are long since dead.

They died three weeks after I last saw them.

The Russians came but this time they couldn't find any men left alive there so they rounded up the women and children, herded them into a circle, covered them in their carefully collected winter stock of dry grass, threw petrol on them and struck a match.

They burnt them alive.

The commander wrote and told me.

He thought that, as a journalist, I could tell this to the world.

I phoned *The Times*, the *Telegraph*. The editors said, 'Where is your proof?'

'There is a pile of bones in Afghanistan, do you want me to go and get them for you?'

'This is Christmas,' they said. 'People only want good news at Christmas.'

I got drunk for a week and cried.

I smashed up my car and cried.

My chimney went on fire and I thought it was a reminder.

The falling soot was shards of blackened clothes.

The sparks were the souls of those I couldn't help.

The express roar of hungry flames were the screams of people no one else could hear.

DIARY ENTRY VII

August 1983
Base Camp, Afghanistan

L IFE in the camp was an ever changing experience of diverse sensations.

It swung between periods of rejuvenating laziness, watching the men play volley ball, chess, listening to, or participating in plans for raids, discussing the various aspects of war, learning how to pull apart and re-assemble kalashnikovs blindfolded, interviewing Mujahideen from different camps, holding lengthy discussions with the *Mullah* (priest) and dodging bombs, bullets, helicopters, and MiGs.

No two days were alike. I did my washing in the river, ate burnt offerings like everyone else, and struggled to contain my dysentery.

Whenever I could, I sat in the shade of a mulberry tree in the courtyard and jotted down what had happened, what was happening, and my feelings.

Sometimes, my mind was so far removed that I wasn't even there.

I also played doctor, whether I wanted to or not. Word had spread like wildfire that Banafsha-Khomar had some medicine and every sunset an endless line of Mujahideen queued up for attention.

God, how I hated myself for my ignorance.

All I had was stomach medicine, aspirin, Savlon, plasters, and bandages.

My meagre supply didn't last long and I resorted to boiled salt water, even though it stung like hell it didn't have quite the same psychological effect as a mystical aluminum foil packed tablet.

One *Mujahid* who came night after night literally tore my heart out.

He was about fourteen, and half of his left foot had been blown away by a mine.

I couldn't do anything except try and clean it while he clenched his teeth, trying unsuccessfully to stem a flow of tears, trying unsuccessfully to prove what a brave man he was.

I cried for him and hoped my tears would act as some form of antiseptic as the single tube of savlon went nowhere. It wasn't meant for a purpose such as this.

I told him to see a doctor, to risk travelling to Pakistan. Somehow, God willing, maybe he could get a horse.

He had to go to a hospital.

He had to have proper treatment, otherwise gangrene would set in.

That child was fourteen, my son would be fourteen one day. That child was fighting a war. I hope my child would never have to.

5. Weapon instruction.

6. Writing letters to loved ones.

7. Playing chess to relieve the stress.

8. Council of war.

The open, running blisters on my own feet attracted flies and threatened to turn septic.

I didn't care.

Salt and water would do for me but what in God's name could I do for these people?

I am ashamed to be a journalist.

I would give my life to have been a doctor even for an hour.

How many lives could I save in one hour?

Lives more worthy of living than my own.

How I hated myself at sunset.

The medicines finished.

Aspirin, Savlon, the stomach medicine, the plasters and bandages I had packed selfishly for myself.

I didn't comprehend the suffering when I made my few purchases in the Inverness branch of Boots the chemist, but even if I had, I could never have brought enough.

God forgive me, I know not what to do.

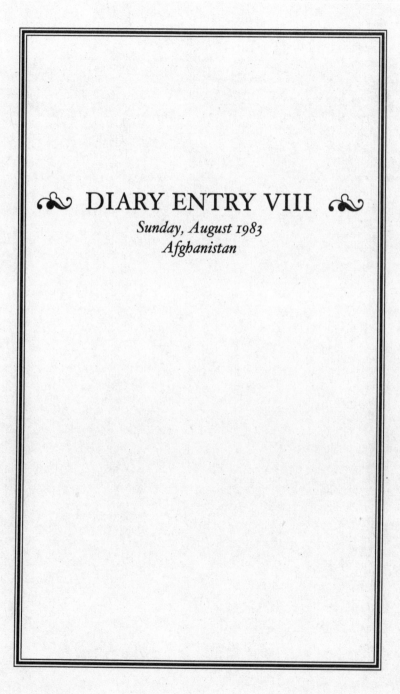

❦ DIARY ENTRY VIII ❦

Sunday, August 1983
Afghanistan

WOKEN by the fly alarm clock at 4:30 a.m.

A lazy stretch on my roof top bed in a heavy dew soaked sleeping bag turned into a fast samba, as the high pitched whine of approaching MiGs broke the peaceful dawn illusion and sent me racing down to the courtyard, colliding with six *Mujahideen* running from the opposite direction.

The MiGs passed overhead. Safe for now.

One raiding party is already out.

Had word of an armoured convoy travelling along the highway on the other side of the mountain.

I wanted to go and join them but the commander left word, 'Not this time.'

Will he come back?

Will the others come back?

When they do, who will be missing?

The tree shading the courtyard is a gun tree.

I call it this because it is used to hang guns and belts of ammunition on, when the *Mujahideen* are in camp.

The gun tree is a mulberry tree.

It is an unearthly tree to be growing here, to make itself available for this purpose.

The sap of a mulberry tree runs in rivers of blood.

Crimson, darkly red, and sticky.

It scares me.

Still, I sit in its shade, leaning my back against it.

The gun tree weeps, everywhere there is a knot it weeps.

It weeps rivers of blood.

The mulberry tree is bleeding now. It bleeds in exactly the same way as the man who had just returned from the raid on the convoy. He has lost the upper part of his right thigh.

The tree bleeds in sympathy.

The man bled to death sometime in the night, but the mulberry tree is still bleeding this morning.

I guess trees take longer to die than men.

There are so many helicopter gunships sailing these skies.

They come in twos, never ones. We can hear the chop, chop, chop of their rotar blades slicing through the stillness for a good ten minutes before they reach us, and then, if we're lucky, for a good ten minutes after they pass over.

I am told they are called 'HINDs' and are equipped with eight machine guns, carry up to one hundred rockets each, and can put a bullet in every square inch for half-a-mile around.

Today, I fired a *Dashaka*, an anti-aircraft gun.

I fired it high into heaven, fired it at a predatory helicopter gunship.

I missed.

The kickback bruised my shoulder.

I didn't think about the man flying the devil's machine when I pulled the trigger. I just aimed, fired, and felt like crying when I missed.

Tomorrow, I'll get one.

As it began to get dark, an expectant hush permeated the camp.

A group of *Mujahideen* gathered around the case of an empty

9. My gun tree in use.

10. The big empty bomb.

1,000 pound bomb.

I know that bomb. It was dropped yesterday.

I saw it falling and thought the end had come.

It was so huge, contained so much death, that there was no point in running.

It bounced harmlessly, crumpling its nose without exploding.

One man died of a heart attack and I wasn't far behind him.

The bomb didn't explode but my bowels did.

Now the *Mujahideen* gather around its empty carcass and talk.

～

It is a meeting of the council.

A meeting of the bomb council and I sit beneath the gun tree and wait.

After a while, they left the bomb and went down to the riverbed.

I went to my rooftop bed, sat, and waited.

I didn't know what I was waiting for, other than supper.

Nothing happened.

I returned to the shelter of the tree.

I am alone.

Suddenly, I hear shouts and the clatter of stones.

I wonder what the hell is happening down by the riverbed until I hear the screams, heart rending screams and shouts.

The clamour of voices.

I know what is happening, but choose not to comprehend it.

I sit under the gun tree, wrapping my veil tightly around myself, against mosquito bites.

I'm on my own, even the cook is not around although supper time is approaching.

I tell myself that, perhaps, it is some religious ceremony.

I try to convince myself that the screaming, the horrific clattering, is anything other than what I know it to be.

I know in my bones what is happening, but the acceptance of it is too much to bear.

These people, many of whom I have come to know and trust and with whom I have developed a reserved kind of friendship, are in the process of stoning someone to death.

Who are they stoning?

Why?

Would they ever stop?

I want to close out the dreadful sounds but am unable to do so.

Stomach churning, adrenalin surging, I huddle closer to the tree for safety.

I watch the stars appear one by one, and pray for silence.

Silence, silence, please God, let them stop throwing stones, let the clatter finish, let the screaming stop.

Please let it be over.

The screams tear the night apart.

The spine chilling clatter, clatter, clatter, clatter of pounding stones, will it ever stop?

Running feet from the opposite end of the camp, sweating, out of breath, guns ready, another group of Mujahideen loom in front of me.

A man shouts from the riverbed, excitement mirrors in the face of two newcomers, and they swiftly stride to join the others.

✍

Pounding, the clatter of stones on flesh.

A voice shouting, another hoarsely screaming.

'What is happening?' the newcomers ask me.

I shake my head.

A man returns from the riverbed and sees me hugging the tree.

'Oh. You heard the noises,' he says in mock surprise. 'It is nothing.'

I keep quiet, wondering who was dead and why.

He explains 'A spy has been caught tonight. He was giving information to the Russians and we caught him. I have never seen him before. I do not know who he is. He is not from here. We hit him. I hit him also.'

The screams stop.

A last couple of stones clatter noisily on to the riverbed, then silence, except for the cicadas, and the cook, now busy with supper.

A spy has just been stoned to death, and they prepare for supper.

One by one, they reappeared from the river bed.

The commander included.

The single oil lamp in the centre of the courtyard cast flickering shadows around the familiar, now unfamiliar faces.

I studied them, wondering at the extremes in their personalities and thanked God that I was on their side.

Islamic law, so different, deeply religious people. It was their way, their judgement, their punishment, and I was so far away from home.

Handsome faces in the lamplight, strong jaws, fine bones, high cheekbones, flashing eyes and teeth.

Flowing movements, strong yet gentle people, smiling, joking, as if nothing had happened. To them, I suppose, nothing had.
For them, this was the way of Islam, it was I, who was out of place, out of time, not them.

It was suppertime.

Everyone sat crosslegged around the dirty oblong, cloth, and washed hands in a bowl with a kettle of water passed round for the purpose.

Five dishes of goat, a feast in this hungry land, piles of nan laid out at intervals.

In the dim light we ate, fingers in mouths, right hand only, into the communal dish.

Two glasses and one pitcher of water were shared too.

I don't know how, but I ate.

What else was there to do?

What had happened had nothing to do with me.

There was nothing I could do to undo what was already part of history.

I daren't say a word, so I sat and ate, studying faces, actions, seeing people in a different light.

The goat was good.

I snuggled back against the gun tree, my spot, my sitting place now and always left vacant for me, sipping a glass of hot, black, heavily sugared tea and listened, not understanding much, just the odd word, now and then.

Lighthearted conversations flowing around the courtyard, backwards and forwards across the small person enclosed space, realizing that I was the only woman in a valley of 1,500 Mujahideen, and it was a good thing that I knew my place.

Later, I sat on my rooftop bed listening to the cicadas, the pounding rhythm of drums echoing from far across the valley.

Then, lying down hands underneath my head, ignoring the whistling dive of the mosquitoes, I watched the heavens mapped out in infinite detail above.

March 1989. Kilcoy, Scotland

I could have slid either way at that moment, slid like a thief in the night towards the border, or slid over the precipitous edge of sanity.

Disassociation, the tool of my survival, a dangerous implement, one, for which I make no excuses for utilizing to the utmost.

If I had at that time, accepted the reality of the stoning, I would have gone mad.

I know that now, and with this knowledge comes the fact that I was already verging on insanity when I undertook the journey. I needed to feel this sharp edge, experience shock and fear, in order to shed my manacles and walk free.

If Afghanistan had been a proverbial Sunday afternoon picnic nothing would have altered the core of my being. I would never have glimpsed the light of day.

Not only was I suddenly a woman, but nurtured by adrenalin pumping fear, I had finally begun to grow.

Fear was the trigger.

The fear of my own inner self.

The fear of what I was capable of.

Man is a killer but no more so than a woman, and I sometimes think that a reckless, distraught, highly emotional woman is far more dangerous than any man.

Perhaps it was the loss of my children which drove me initially, but this widened to include images of the dispossessed, images of horrifically injured people, images of the dead and dying, images of bombed out homes and burning crops, images of MiGs and helicopters, images of the atrocities committed against one human being by another.

Yes, I've shot at planes, I've shot at men and hit them too, but that doesn't make me any more or any less of a person.

Unexpected situations result in unexpected reactions, and actions perpetrated in the anguished heat of the moment are done, finished, ended, although memories surface in day-mares and screaming nightmares.

We can't go back but only forward into a new day with new beginnings.

I can write all this now, after all, this is 1989 and that was 1983.

Strangely enough, I've never been able to take myself back over that particular border before and, in doing so now, can begin to come to terms with the past, for that's what it is, the past.

I suppose writing is a form of therapy.

DIARY ENTRY IX

Monday, 29 August 1983
Afghanistan

MIGS and reconnaissance planes passing overhead, anti-aircraft guns firing.

How long until the next bombing run on our camp?

Two helicopters.

The most unnerving sound on earth.

We hear the ominous chop, chop, chop of slashing blades long before they get here, sit and wait, and wait, and wait, Are they coming for us or will they fly over?

Sitting against the tree, waiting.

Everyone poised for action, suddenly diving for guns, for anything, they are close, too close.

I get as far as judging how many seconds to reach the bomb shelter, but never actually move, just watch and listen.

The helicopters are circling now.

The tattoo of anti-aircraft guns is deafening.

I can almost make out the faces of the pilots.

Mujahideen are firing kalashnikovs.

Any second now.

Fingers reach for triggers.

Fire...fire...fire...

❧

Why am I sitting here scribbling in my notebook?

Grab a gun.

Try to get them first.

I can't move.

My legs won't move.

I don't believe it!

They're going!

I can breathe. Are they coming back?

Chop, chop, chop.

Fading into the distance.

'Banafsha-Khomar...You didn't run,' said the commander smiling.

I smiled back and lit a cigarette.

I couldn't find a voice to speak

 DIARY ENTRY X

Tuesday, 30 August 1983
Afghanistan

11. Banafsha-Khomar.

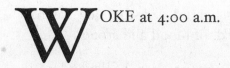WOKE at 4:00 a.m.

Sun rising between distant mountain peaks.

Sun on one side, silver moon still glowing on the other, I sit on a rope bed on an adobe rooftop in between.

Prayer time's over.

Firewood being chopped for the kitchen.

Wood smoke curling skywards, blue and tangy.

Breakfast over.

I am told that I am going with the commander up into the mountains to bring down ammunition from an underground store.

'Banafsha-Khomar. Come', with the wave of an imperious finger.

'Horse.'

There are ten of us but only the commander and I are on horseback, each leading a baggage pony on a long reign fastened to the back of the saddle.

We rode up the dry riverbed, leaving it a couple of hours later to begin the upward climb.

One in front, one behind, side by side we rode down a dried up riverbed, of blood and stones.

•

Rode through an open pasture of lavender, its pungent aroma released under the steady trampling of hooves.

Entered the beginning of a long, narrow gorge, real Wild West stuff, Grand Canyon.

Sentries outlined against the narrow blue ribbon of the sky above, waving down to us, firing shots in the air, true cowboy style.

Ricochet, ricochet, reverberating from cliff to cliff.

Riding up a magical corridor full of butterflies, blue, red, yellow, orange splashed wings.

The sound of hooves ringing on rock.

The climb got progressively steeper and narrower, then, unexpectedly we were out in the open.

A secret valley nestling green and verdant between orange and pink toned cliffs.

A welcoming volley of anti-aircraft fire and loud yipees when we arrived at a small cluster of adobe huts.

The ammunition was stored in small caches in scattered caves at the base of the cliffs.

12. A moment's respite.

13. In my charge.

14. Ammunition camp gun tree.

Certainly a safe place, as the canyon is so narrow that helicopters would have great difficulty in getting in.

They would have to manoeuvre in below the top of the cliffs which are interspersed with anti-aircraft gun positions.

&

Apparently, the gorge was once mined.

The commander's brother was killed there.

His photograph is nailed to this camp's gun tree.

A walnut tree, this one, not a mulberry.

We have to go back the same way.

&

Everyone gathers in the shade of the tree.

Time to relax, swap stories, and drink endless cups of tea.

For once, my presence isn't merely tolerated.

I am actually included in the conversation, and asked so many questions that my head spins.

Why was I here? This question carries the most weight, and one which I answered haltingly, under the impenetrable gaze of twenty pairs of eyes.

I must have said the right thing as afterwards they lined up to shake my hand.

What news, if any, reached the West and, what did people there think of the situation? What did I think of the situation? What would happen in the long run?

What would I tell people when I returned?

In the soporific heat and creeping laziness, I attempt to sound intelligent.

Lengthy discussions about minerals, natural gas fields, military strategy, and the concept of bandits continues in an unabated, passionate torrent, while the sun climbs majestically towards its zenith.

Conversation only flags when mouths become dry, and more tea is demanded.

A dusty purple cushion is produced from somewhere and thrown towards me.

We drink tea.

I doze and they play a leisurely game of chess while bombs pound in the distance.

Shoulders shrug at the incessant bombing.

What could we do except listen, and try to blot out the horrific images of what we had seen and would see again.

I took off my watch and my skin came with it. This was nothing compared to the other things happening elsewhere as we sat, and sat, and sat.

It was late afternoon before we made a move to leave.

We were safe here and I, for one, didn't relish the thought of travelling back.

The commander rode one horse and I, the other, each of us escorting a pack-pony laden with anti-tank missiles and klashnikovs.

The others, who had come with us from the base camp, carried what they could on their backs and in their arms.

We wound our way back down the ravine, wary of mines, the commander humming softly under his breath, occasionally breaking out into full fledged songs. I think they were hymns.

I sang too... just whatever came into my head.

We laughed a lot.

Had interesting conversation in a mixture of three languages.

We even managed an impromptu horse race.

❧

Waving an arm towards distant mountains, he rhymed off place names, told me where 'Bomb-bombs' had fallen, where there were no people left, which crops grew, the names of birds and plants.

Picked me a flower, a *Banafsha*, a cornflower blue daisy, that grows wild in the mountains of Afghanistan.

I thwacked the backside of his horse, it reared and he fell off.

He took me to meet some women, a small farmstead, where shy girls hid in the small house, and an old lady came and sat with us on a rug beneath a heavily laden pomegranate tree.

We ate unripe apricots, hot nan, fresh yoghurt, and pomegranates from the tree.

We continued our journey all too soon.

Rode back down the dried up riverbed where brambles ripened and geese flew overhead reminding me of home.

An old man, half crippled, wearing plastic sandals, and balancing himself on a walking stick, with unkempt hair and beard, bloody upper lip and infected, fly encrusted nose, waited for us.

The commander examined him unflinchingly.

He asked me if I had any medicine.

I didn't.

They spoke for a few minutes more and the old man was sent towards the farmstead, I think.

We rode on in silence.

Each thinking our own private thoughts.

Two MiGs roared into view.

We hurried into the trees.

Anti-aircraft guns fired.

The planes left.

We continued.

Two helicopter gunships now.

More gunfire.

We didn't laugh anymore.

We were back.

❧ DIARY ENTRY XI ❧

Wednesday, 31 August 1983
Afghanistan

WOKE to the sound of migrating geese, a 'V' across the dawning heavens.

Rose, brushed and plaited my hair to the rattling thunder of anti-aircraft guns, slipped on my sandals to the rhythm of rotar blades, washed my face in the irrigation ditch to the roar of MiGs , and knew that today the camp was going to be hit.

As we sat in the courtyard quietly finishing breakfast, the sound of bombing came closer.

'Somewhere in the valley,' said the commander.

We drank tea, expressions fixed, listening to the bombing growing closer.

No one moved.

Apprehensively waiting for action.

Silence, the sound of anti-aircraft guns, silence.

Two helicopters, tension mounting, anti-aircraft guns, silence.

Bombs exploding, men reaching for guns, unhurried, tense, watching, listening, waiting, waiting, waiting, silence.

Slowly relaxing.

Conversations reopening.

Eating.

Drinking tea.

Anti-aircraft guns, bombs exploding, earth trembling, silence.

Worried glances exchanged.

An earthquake in the pit of my stomach.

Bombs exploding.

Cold cramps.

May be this was it.

May be today it would end, for me at least.

Bombs exploding.

Anti-aircraft guns firing, silence, silence.

More bombs.

Wish they'd get it over with.

Two MiGs overhead, us just waiting our turn.

Just a matter of time but the knowing and waiting is nerve wracking.

Helicopters now, and those damned anti-aircraft guns are working overtime.

The commander had just told me to pack.

He says I am to leave now.

I refuse,

&

Shrugging his shoulders in an apologetic manner, he says, 'No, Banafsha-Khomar, the Russians are coming again. Today there is a camp. This morning there is a camp. This morning we are here. One hour, two hours, they come and,' he opened his hands and his life ran through them.

'Banafsha-Khomar. You go. You will come back. But now you go.'

There was no way to argue.

I slowly walked the long way round to my rooftop bed, thoughts in a whirl.

Rolled up my sleeping bag.

Stuffed my few belongings haphazardly into my pack.

Retraced my steps to the courtyard and tried not to cry.

I wouldn't break now.

&

Three of the commander's cousins had been told to take me back to Pakistan. None of us wanted to go, but orders were orders.

Stumbling on foot, up the stony sand hot hillside I wanted to turn around but couldn't.

When we finally reached the top of the slope though, I gave in.

I had to look.

The camp was a magnet and I just had to look back.

It spread out beneath me.

I knew it was there, camouflaged by trees with the occasional open space.

There was the volley ball pitch.

There was my rooftop.

There, standing alone by the big empty bomb, was a solitary figure with a hand raised in farewell.

An hour later, one of my sandal straps snapped, and I continued barefoot.

I didn't feel the pain of jagged rocks piercing my skin. Other pains were much more acute.

෴

Walked on in complete silence.

Buried in thoughts and emotions.

Thinking of how soon I would return.

How much help I would bring.

Ignoring the MiGs, helicopters, anti-aircraft gunfire, and distant bombing.

There was a horse for me at the farmstead along with smiles from the old woman, and giggles from the girls.

I wanted to stay with them.

'No', said the commander's cousins. 'Pakistan'.

෴

We seemed to reach the top of the first mountain in no time at all and, as we paused momentarily, to look back the way we had come, three MiGs in a 'V' formation, flew low out of the sun.

They banked in a half circle to descend fast, dark, ominous towards the head of the valley.

Then dived in a wheezing, screaming, terrifying bombing run, days overdue by all counts.

My blood froze and my heart stood still.

We stood there.

Silent spectators.

So small, so vulnerable, so helpless.

Listening to the sound of explosions.

Picturing the camp.

Picturing friends.

The faces, ah, those faces.

Seeing them running, reaching for useless guns, racing for shelter through showers of fragmenting masonry, blasts of bone stripping sand, jagged splinters bursting from shrapnel bombs, tearing into limbs.

Blood dripping from the gun tree.

Roof top beds falling, buildings crumbling, desperate confusion, desperate situation, desperate men, and the commander standing alone by the big bomb, hand raised in farewell.

The MiGs came back into view.

Birds of doom speeding away on a wave of destruction and death. Five helicopter gunships moved in.

I knew that by the time we descended the first mountain, and long before we began to climb the next, the tanks would be in what little was left of the camp.

If anyone was left alive, the fighting would be fierce. I could already hear the screams of the wounded and dying. I could already see the faces of the dead.

The three men prayed as we descended the mountain.

I fought not to scream, not to turn and race back towards something I could neither change nor help.

We halted by a small pool of water.

The men washed, then prayed again.

I washed, then prayed too.

⁊

The sun began its crimson journey into night as we rode through pastures of lavender and miniature white roses into the village of women and children.

The children, colourful butterflies, ran to greet me.

The women stood outside their homes, erect and proud, they waved me on my way.

That night I slept on another rooftop.

I lay watching the shooting stars, each one the soul of a dead *Mujahid*, each one, carrying the name of a friend.

A quick burst of rifle fire close by, a scurry of night time activity.

I hoped they'd finally come for me.

I waited to welcome death but it stayed away.

 DIARY ENTRY XII

Thursday, 1 September 1983
Afghanistan

The journey was rapid.

The pace exhausting.

The sun scorching.

The mountains forbidding.

We picked our way across minefields.

Rode through burning crops and smouldering villages.

We were no longer alone.

The way out was marked by a steady stream of refugees.

'No,' I wasn't a doctor.

'No,' I didn't have medicines.

'Yes,' I would return.

'Yes,' I was going to get help.

'Yes,' I had seen.

As we moved out of one village, the Russians moved in behind us.

There was no way back now.

Tanks rumbled.

Rockets soared and fell, scattering death and mutilation.

I didn't have a gun anymore,

I had left it in the camp.

Women and children were being murdered behind me.

I had no gun but I did have bare hands.

I turned my horse to the village and galloped headlong towards the hell.

One of my bodyguards galloped alongside me and as we argued about the futility of going back, the angry whizz of a sniper bullet cut deftly through the air so close to my head that I tasted the fear of death which I had naively thought was gone.

My companion pushed me down low over the horse's neck.

Reins torn from between my clenched fingers and gone.

Caught in a deadly crossfire of bullets and rockets, and a barrage of screams, we hurled ourselves across the open space between fields, low walls, bombed out homes, and an exploding minefield.

We reached the other side, galloped some more, then stopped, gasping for breath.

I tried to light a cigarette.

My hands were shaking too much.

I dropped it.

&

As darkness approached, we crawled towards the border, the tide of refugees swelling at each step.

The women held their veils close.

The children walked, or were carried, in silence.

The men shuffled their feet and carried what they could.

As we reached the final stretch, night closed in.

I stopped my horse, turned in the saddle, and looked back.

One last look at the purple fading mountains, the sombre clad cedar slopes, prayer flags fluttering in the wind, pictures of hoplessness, of forgotten peace, of friends made, friends lost, images of a war that was my war now.

Finally, I allowed myself the untold luxury of silent tears.

It was dark. No one could see me. I could no longer see them.

The endless caravan of tears crossed the border into Pakistan.

Their faces were haunted, their pain intense.

The wounded, the dying, and the living dead, reaching for the comparative safety of refugee status.

Some of them even made it.

I know.

I was one.